P9-AZW-345

The TRAVELS of BENJAMIN of TUDELA

THROUGH THREE CONTINENTS IN THE TWELFTH CENTURY

Uri Shulevitz

Farrar Straus Giroux
New York

*T*o the John Simon Guggenheim Memorial Foundation for making the research for this book possible and enabling me to follow in Benjamin's footsteps part of the way, and to the memory of Roger W. Straus.

I wish also to thank all those who have helped me directly or indirectly on this project and all those I might have unintentionally omitted; thanks to all my friends at FSG, especially to my editor, Margaret Ferguson, for her patience, encouragement, and dedication; to Elaine Chubb, the copy editor, for her careful reading of the manuscript and her most helpful suggestions; to Ehud Ben Ezer; Dennis Brown; Professor Eli Yassif, Tel Aviv University; Professor Yafa Berlowitz, Tel Aviv University; Edna Heichal, IFA, Haifa University; Julio Ramón Segura Moneo, municipal archivist, Tudela, Spain; Karen Cushman; James Craig; Lloyd Glasson; Donna Brooks; Rena Messer; Margaret Dennis; Barbara Roberts; the librarians, especially Kathryn Franco, at the James M. Milne Library, State University of New York College at Oneonta; Karen Coeman; Dan Almagor; Professor Dov Noy, Jerusalem; and Ruth Porter, Museum of the Jewish Diaspora, Tel Aviv University. Last but not least, my thanks to Paula Brown, for her generous help and support.

Copyright © 2005 by Uri Shulevitz. All rights reserved. Distributed in Canada by Douglas & McIntyre Ltd. Color separations by Chroma Graphics PTE Ltd. Printed and bound in China by South China Printing Co. Ltd. First edition, 2005.

3   5   7   9   10   8   6   4   2

www.fsgkidsbooks.com

Library of Congress Cataloging-in-Publication Data

Shulevitz, Uri, date.
   The travels of Benjamin of Tudela : through three continents in the twelfth century / Uri Shulevitz.—1st ed.
      p.   cm.
   Summary: A fictionalized account of the travels of Benjamin, a Jewish man from Tudela, Spain, who, in 1159, set out on a fourteen-year-long journey that took him to Italy, Greece, Palestine, Persia, Egypt, and Sicily.
   ISBN-13: 978-0-374-37754-0
   ISBN-10: 0-374-37754-5
   1. Benjamin, of Tudela, 12th cent.—Juvenile fiction.   [1. Benjamin, of Tudela, 12th cent.—Fiction.   2. Jews—History—Fiction.   3. Middle Ages—Fiction.   4. Travelers—Fiction.   5. Voyages and travels—Fiction.]   I. Title.

PZ7.S5574Tr 2005
[Fic]—dc22
                                                                                                2004040434

It is 1173.

A traveler hurries along a road that is barely visible. It is covered with thick layers of soil, stones, and broken branches. He pulls down his wide-brimmed hat to shield his eyes from the setting sun. From time to time, his feet sink in mud.

He is weary. But he must hurry. The road is long; the day is short. He must reach Tudela, a town in northern Spain, before the town gates are locked for the night. He tightens his grip on the large staff in his hand and walks faster.

Dusk.

He has arrived too late. The gates are shut. Small groups are gathered by the town walls. They must all now wait for the gates to open at dawn.

Some of the people have made fires to keep warm. The traveler collects wood, pulls flint stones from his large leather pouch, and sparks a fire. He takes out bread, cuts a piece of cheese with his knife, and has supper. He washes it down with water from his leather flask. Then he wraps himself in his long cloak and sits leaning against a rock, his staff next to him.

To sleep is dangerous. He may be attacked by wild beasts or by robbers. A night of sleep is short; a sleepless night is endless.

Daybreak.

From Tudela's highest tower the watchman's horn is heard announcing dawn. Drowsy, bleary-eyed, the traveler hears the creaking of the heavy town gates opening slowly.

A line of people forms by the gates. When the traveler's turn comes, he shows the guards his papers. Then he pays the toll and enters Tudela.

The traveler heads toward the Jewish quarter. He negotiates his way through narrow, dirty streets. He is careful not to step on rotting garbage, dead rats, and animal manure. The stench is strong. He walks close to the walls to avoid being showered by garbage and by the contents of chamber pots that housemaids empty from windows.

He enters the synagogue. The old rabbi studies his face and gray beard and says, "Stranger, you remind me of a man I once knew. Who are you?"

"Rabbi," the traveler replies, "I'm Benjamin, son of Jonah."

"Praise be to God!" exclaims the old rabbi. "You've come home."

The news spreads quickly. "Benjamin is here!"

That very evening a supper is given to celebrate Benjamin's safe return. "We thought you'd never come back," says one person. "We thought you were dead," says another.

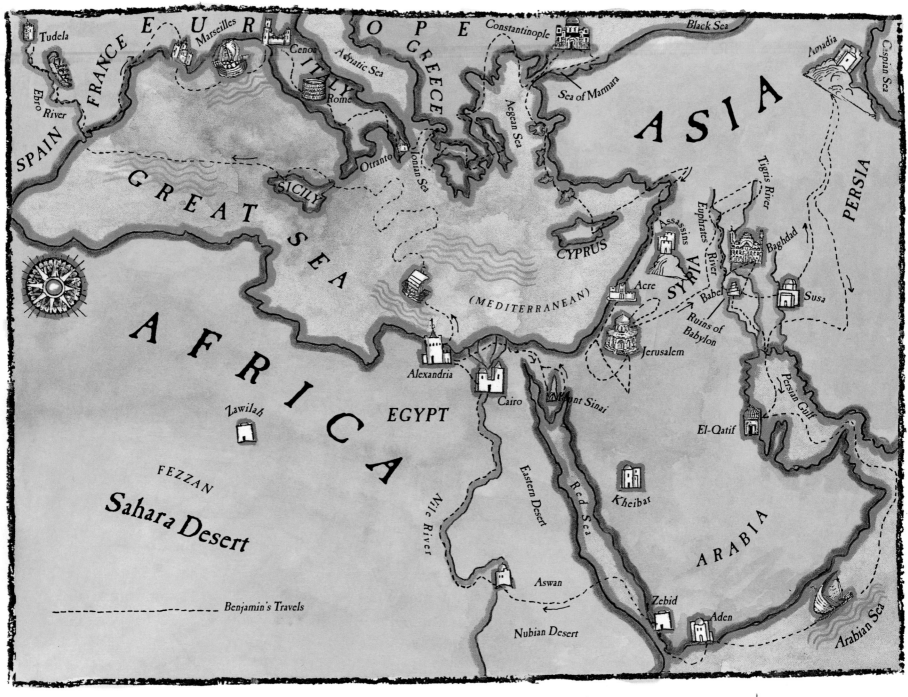

*I*n 1159, more than one hundred years before Marco Polo's travels, Benjamin had left his native town of Tudela in northern Spain to travel throughout the then-known world.

*D*ear friends, says Benjamin, as most of you know, I'd always dreamed of seeing Jerusalem, and as many places mentioned in the Bible as possible. I could find no peace until my dreams became reality.

I know that when I decided to leave Tudela fourteen years ago, to abandon the comforts of home for the hardships and dangers of the unknown, some of you thought I'd gone mad. Do you remember how you tried to talk me out of going on a journey from which few ever return alive? Do you remember how some of you mourned me, as if I were already dead? True, some of you also wished you could join me.

Now you ask: Was my journey difficult? Yes, it was. Was it dangerous? Yes, very. In spite of it all, am I glad I went? Yes, I am.

If I told you of every place I've been to, of all I've seen—the companions I've traveled with, the people I've met, or the lonely days; the exotic foods I've tasted, or the times I went hungry and cold; the soaking rains and burning suns, the beautiful sights and arid deserts—my story would be almost as long as my journey.

So I'll tell you only about the most amazing places I saw and the most fascinating stories I heard.

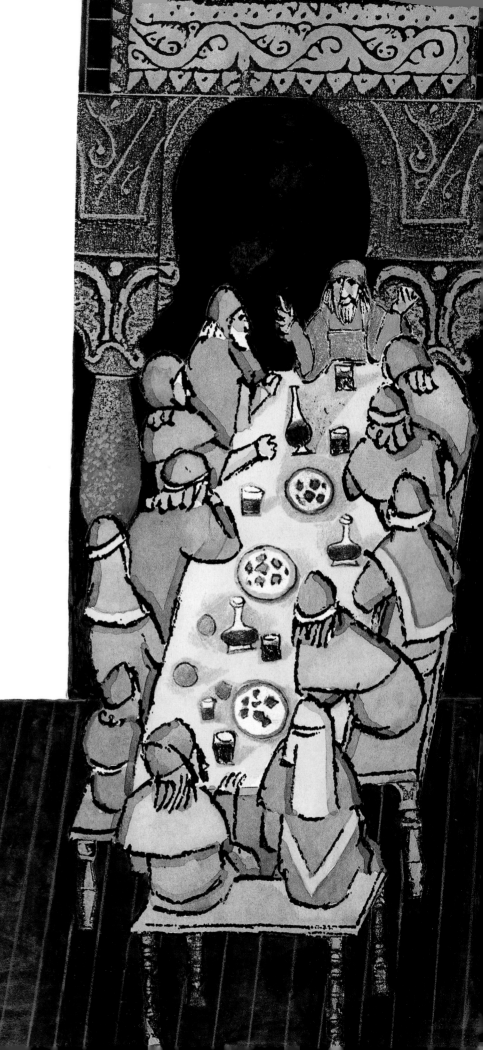

The JOURNEY BEGINS

The papers a traveler might carry consisted of a receipt from his hometown's authorities that he had paid his taxes, and a letter requesting safe passage and testifying to his worthiness, that he owed no debts in his community, and that he was not running away from justice. Benjamin might also have carried a letter of credit, to receive money advances in Jewish communities along his journey, to be repaid by him, upon his return to Tudela, or by his family, in case of his death. These letters were safer and lighter than the heavy coins of his day, and they were of no use to robbers who couldn't read.

I remember the day I set out as if it were yesterday. It was a chilly spring dawn. I was full of excitement and apprehension. I checked one more time to make sure I had all my papers, my knife, flints, food, extra stockings.

When I was ready, I embarked on a small barge on the Ebro River that would take me to the Great Sea. Travel by water is faster than by land, but far from comfortable. The barge creaked and swayed as we went southeast on the river. It was crammed with merchants and their goods—sacks of salt and needles, casks of wine and oil—and peasants with chickens, a pig, and a goat. I could barely move my knees or my arms to scratch my beard. The goat took a particular liking to me, perhaps because we both had beards—or was it because I shared some of my food with him?

We stopped periodically, which enabled us to stretch our legs on land. At night we slept on the shore near the barge.

In four days we reached the Great Sea.

After traveling along the Spanish coast, I headed for the French port of Marseilles. I traveled many days by foot and by wagon. The wagon was drawn by oxen. Like the barge, it was packed with people and goods, but it was much slower. The ride was rough, over bumpy roads.

When you travel, it is vital to be able to understand and be understood. Luckily, I speak several languages. Traveling companions advised me to praise the host country and scorn its enemies. They also taught me some useful phrases in various tongues. But sometimes I had to manage with sign language.

I reached Marseilles at sunset. The streets were growing dark. I hired a boy with a torch to take me to the guesthouse next to the synagogue in the Jewish quarter. He knew the city and guided me through streets in which I was less likely to be attacked by cutthroats and thieves, who roam the night looking for easy prey.

By BARGE,
by FOOT, *by* WAGON,
by SHIP

The next morning I went to the harbor. I inquired about a ship going to Genoa, in Italy, only to find out that I had just missed one. And so I learned that no ship waits for you, but you have to wait for a ship.

Every day at dawn I went down through the winding streets to the harbor. I inquired, and I waited. At dusk I returned to the guesthouse for the night, only to repeat the same the next day, and the next. After I had waited for three weeks, a ship bound for Genoa finally came. Then we waited another week for favorable winds. This was to be my first sea voyage.

When I boarded the ship, the captain was shouting curses at the drunken crew, who were loading barrels and sacks. I climbed down a steep, narrow ladder into the ship's hold. Only a faint light filtered in from the upper deck, so day and night it was dark. My eyes were unaccustomed to this darkness, and I bumped into my fellow passengers. All of us were to share these cramped quarters. It was hot. Rat urine had soaked into the boat's wooden boards. The smell was overwhelming.

The captain shouted commands. The sailors hoisted the sails. At last we were off. The houses and the harbor grew smaller and the sea grew larger. For the first time in my life, I had a feeling of the vastness of the world.

That night, lying on a thin layer of straw on the floor, I couldn't sleep. It was so crowded that there was no room to stretch my legs. I listened to the constant groaning of the ship as the waves crashed against it. Each wave reminded me how small and helpless I was, and how big and powerful the sea was. I wondered if I'd be alive in the morning, or at the bottom of the sea. The ship's constant rocking made me feel seasick. I climbed over the other passengers and went to the upper deck. The fresh air was a relief.

I had my own food—bread, cheese, nuts, and dried fruit. Those who didn't had to eat the ship's maggot-infested food—or eat nothing. We all drank foul-tasting water. As a result, many of the passengers had to run to the deck to be sick.

After four days that felt like four weeks, I could see in the distance the high towers of Genoa.

I was happy to reach land, but anxious to continue my journey. Since it was risky traveling alone, I always tried to join a group of travelers going my way. And so I left Genoa on foot with several others and set out for Rome.

The closer I got to Rome, the more people I came across heading there for different reasons. There were travelers going to see the Pope: pilgrims to be blessed, penitents to be forgiven for their sins, long files of cripples hoping for a miracle cure, blind men tapping the road with their staffs, clergymen, and monks. There were knights and noblemen on horseback, and soldiers on foot—all on their way to Rome. Merchants with packhorses and donkeys loaded with goods to sell in the marketplace. Beggars and vagrants with menacing faces.

ROME
The WEEPING COLUMNS

In ancient times, Rome was a city-state, which gradually became an empire, ruling over most of the then-known world, until its fall in the fifth century A.D., after about one thousand years of existence.

I entered the city gate. Rome is big—like countless Tudelas rolled into one. I passed by the most beautiful palaces and churches, among them the Pope's palace. The streets were filled with vendors hawking their wares at the top of their voices—the soap and needle sellers the loudest—while merchants tapped wine bowls with small sticks, announcing the latest wine arrivals. Church bells rang, donkeys brayed, horses neighed, voices chattered—all these sounds blended into one loud, deafening noise that echoed between the buildings.

I left the noisy streets behind and headed to the Colosseum, and then to the Forum. The Roman ruins, the columns and arches, stood in an open space, in total silence. I wandered alone, in awe of these relics of the ancient past. But when I reached the Arch of Titus, which celebrates Titus's conquest of Jerusalem more than a thousand years ago, and saw the carvings of Roman soldiers carrying the sacred seven-branched menorah from the holy Temple in Jerusalem, I was filled with deep sadness. It was victory for Rome, but for us a loss of our homeland and the beginning of our exile.

That evening my hosts told me a most amazing story: When Titus returned to Rome from Jerusalem, he also brought back two bronze columns from the holy Temple. These columns are now in the church of St. John Lateran. Every year, on the anniversary of the destruction of the Temple, a miracle happens: the columns exude moisture, as if weeping.

The first Temple in Jerusalem—the renowned Solomon's Temple—was destroyed by the Babylonians in 586 B.C., on the ninth day of the Hebrew month of Av. The Temple was rebuilt and it was destroyed by Titus, the Roman Emperor-to-be, in A.D. 70, 656 years to the day from its original destruction. The destruction of the Temple was the greatest tragedy in ancient times of the Jewish people, and the ninth day of Av the saddest day on their calendar.

From Rome, I had intended to go straight to Jerusalem. But after hearing about Constantinople, the largest, the wealthiest, and the most beautiful city in all of Christendom, I decided to go there first.

I headed south from Rome to the seaport of Otranto. First my traveling companions and I crossed the mountains. We had to climb up and down barely visible paths, watching for loose boulders and falling rocks, careful not to slip and fall into an abyss. I was never sure what to expect at every turn of the narrow, twisting path—robbers or wild animals. Then we walked along the coast, south to Otranto. From there I took a ship through the Ionian Sea.

W e sailed along the coast so we wouldn't get lost. I was enjoying this voyage—the sea was calm and the weather was beautiful.

Then one morning two pirate ships appeared out of nowhere. We were terrified. If pirates catch you, they cut off your ears and nose and make you a slave. Or, if you are lucky, they hold you for ransom. They chased us, but with the help of God and the skill of our navigator, we managed to lose them. But our troubles were not over. Now we were off course, and there were no winds. It was hot. We were running out of drinking water and were in danger of dying of thirst. We drifted helplessly for several days.

Finally, favorable winds blew, and we resumed our journey. When we reached the coast of a Greek island, the local people refused to give us fresh water and threatened to kill us. As I found out the hard way, strangers are not welcome. Whether they believed we had a contagious disease or we brought bad luck, I'll never know. We had no choice but to continue on our way without water. Luckily, it rained and we managed to collect rainwater.

At last, we reached the Greek mainland. From there I continued by land and by sea to Constantinople.

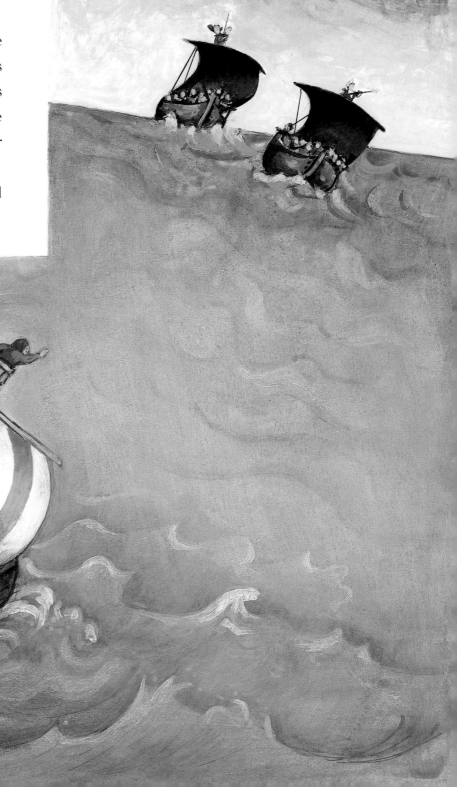

PIRATES

CONSTANTINOPLE
The CHRISTMAS SPECTACLE

Constantinople was named in honor of Emperor Constantine. It was the capital of the Byzantine Empire from A.D. 330 until its fall in 1453. It was the seat of the head of the Eastern Christians, who didn't obey the Pope of Rome.

When our ship approached Constantinople, I saw a city rising majestically from the sea, gleaming in the morning sun. We sailed past the city walls, which were built seven hundred years ago and have withstood countless attacks. Towering over the walls was a mountain of colors—palaces, churches, houses with shining rooftops. When we reached the harbor, ships from as far away as Russia, Spain, and Egypt were anchored there. I knew I was about to enter the wealthiest, most powerful city of Europe.

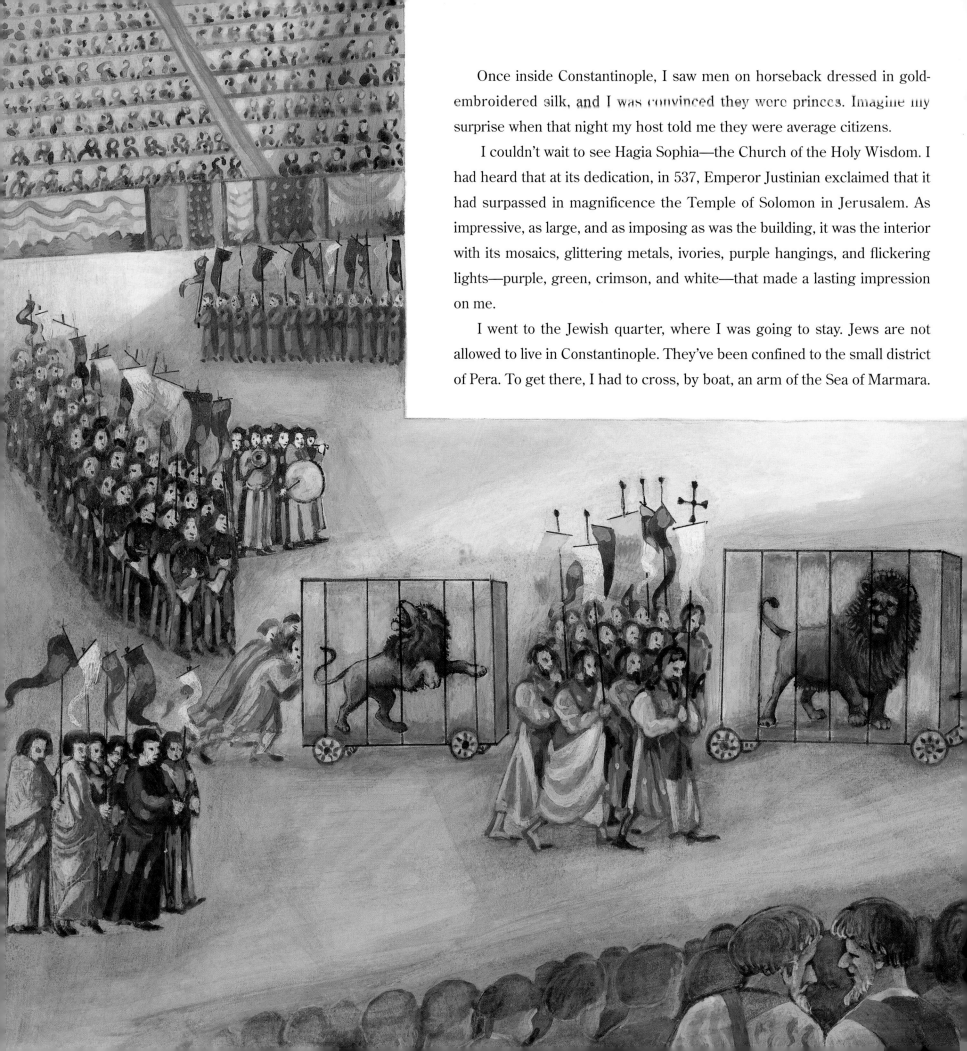

Once inside Constantinople, I saw men on horseback dressed in gold-embroidered silk, and I was convinced they were princes. Imagine my surprise when that night my host told me they were average citizens.

I couldn't wait to see Hagia Sophia—the Church of the Holy Wisdom. I had heard that at its dedication, in 537, Emperor Justinian exclaimed that it had surpassed in magnificence the Temple of Solomon in Jerusalem. As impressive, as large, and as imposing as was the building, it was the interior with its mosaics, glittering metals, ivories, purple hangings, and flickering lights—purple, green, crimson, and white—that made a lasting impression on me.

I went to the Jewish quarter, where I was going to stay. Jews are not allowed to live in Constantinople. They've been confined to the small district of Pera. To get there, I had to cross, by boat, an arm of the Sea of Marmara.

Since winter was approaching, making a long sea voyage treacherous, I decided to stay in Pera and see more of Constantinople. I went to the annual Christmas spectacle in the Hippodrome—the world-famous place of amusement in Constantinople—which is near the Imperial Palace. I saw long processions of men leading lions, leopards, bears, and wild birds, to perform fights, magic tricks, and jugglery. In all my travels I haven't seen anything anywhere else to compare.

When spring came, I left for Jerusalem. Again I traveled by ship, through the Greek islands to Cyprus. After my Ionian Sea experience, I was worried about pirates, but we reached Cyprus peacefully. Once there, however, I was forced to wait for several months because of an epidemic of the plague that was raging on the mainland. When the epidemic passed, I was finally able to leave Cyprus.

The ASSASSINS

About a hundred years after Benjamin's journey, the Assassin strongholds were captured by Mameluke Turks in 1273, ending their reign of terror.

Next I went through Syria. Because of the great heat, I traveled at night and slept during the day. Yes, it was easier to travel at night and avoid the heat, but it was safer, too. The truth is, I was scared. I wasn't the only one afraid—all the people in this area live in fear because there is so much fighting between Christian Crusaders and Muslims, but in particular because of the threat of the Assassins. It was safer to travel under the cover of darkness.

You see, ruthless killers could come down anytime from their inaccessible fortresses high up on the mountains. The Hashishin, or Assassins, blindly obey their prophet—the Old Man of the Mountain—and are willing to die for him. Their prophet sends them, while they are under the influence of hashish, to assassinate kings, Christian Crusaders, and even fellow Muslims.

You can imagine my deep relief when I reached Acre, a small town but an important port. It is the gateway to the Land of Israel and Jerusalem, its capital. Everybody—pilgrims and Christian Crusaders who sail from Europe to continue by land to Jerusalem—comes here.

Christian Crusaders, mostly from France, rule Acre. They're disliked because they look down upon Muslims, Jews, and even other Christians—Syrian Christians, Georgian Christians, and the Greek Orthodox.

The CRUSADERS

Christian Crusaders came from Europe to capture the Land of Israel from the Muslims. In 1099, after a bitter battle, they took Jerusalem, which had been under Muslim rule since the seventh century A.D., and massacred Muslims and Jews. Witnesses said that rivers of blood flowed through the streets of Jerusalem.

JERUSALEM

The SECRET TOMBS of the ANCIENT HEBREW KINGS

The Jewish nation lived in their homeland, the Land of Israel, for over one thousand years, until A.D. 70, when the Romans destroyed Jerusalem.

I approached Jerusalem with awe. At the sight of the city I tore the corner of my garment, as is the Jewish custom, in memory of the destruction of the Temple, and I wept. Jerusalem, holy to our forefathers, once the capital of the kingdom of the Jewish people . . . My friends, I was stunned. Jerusalem was so different from my dreams. This city, so important to Jews, to Christians, and to Muslims—which every map shows as the center of the world—is so small! It doesn't compare in size or splendor to Rome or Constantinople.

Fortified by three walls, Jerusalem now has very few Jews—a mere two hundred. It is mostly full of Christian Crusader knights, who rule the city.

I met the pious and reclusive Rabbi Abraham of Constantinople. He told me the following story:

On Mount Zion, one of the hills in Jerusalem, are the tombs of the ancient Hebrew kings. There are no buildings there except for a church.

Fifteen years ago there was an earthquake, and a wall of the church collapsed. The Christian Patriarch hired workers to rebuild it. Among the workers were two friends. One day the friends came to work late. To make up for lost time, they continued working after the others had gone home.

The two friends were gathering stones for rebuilding the wall. When they removed a large stone, they discovered the opening of a cave. They entered the cave to see if any money was there. As they continued inside, they came to a magnificent palace. When they tried to enter the palace, a powerful wind, like a tempest, knocked them to the ground. There they lay, as if dead, until nightfall.

Then another wind shouted in a powerful man's voice, "Get up and get out!" The men were frightened and ran away as fast as they could.

They went to the Patriarch and told him what had happened. He consulted Rabbi Abraham. The rabbi knew these must be the tombs of the ancient Hebrew kings. He said to the Patriarch, "Let's have the workers take us there tomorrow."

The next morning, when the Patriarch and Rabbi Abraham went to get the workers, they found them terror-stricken. They refused to return to the cave and cried, "God does not wish this place to be known!"

The Christian Patriarch understood it was sacred ground and should not be trespassed upon. He had the cave sealed and hidden so that no one could find the exact location of the tombs of the ancient Hebrew kings.

Rabbi Abraham told me all this.

*I*n spite of the hardships and dangers, my desire to travel wasn't weakened. I headed on to Babylonia, and to the great city of Baghdad, which is not only the center of Arab culture and the seat of the Caliph, the Arab king and religious leader, but also the residence of the head of all the Jewish communities in this part of the world.

It was dangerous to travel as a European through Muslim lands, because of the war between the Christian Crusaders and the Muslims. So, to be safe, I spent this part of my trip dressed as an Arab. I spoke Arabic, I sat on the ground when I ate, and I followed all the local customs.

I traveled north by way of Damascus, toward the great rivers Euphrates and Tigris, to Baghdad. It took me nearly two months, by camel, donkey, and riverboat, to get there.

BAGHDAD

The CELEBRATION of EL-ID-BED-RAMAZAN

In Benjamin's day, only Constantinople was comparable in size to Baghdad. Baghdad was founded in A.D. 762 as the new capital of the caliphate. The Caliph is the successor, or literally the "substitute," of the prophet Muhammad. He is both the king and the religious leader of the Muslims.

When I entered Baghdad, the outside walls of the houses were decorated with silk and purple cloth. I heard the sound of men and women singing and rejoicing.

I asked an old gentleman in my best Arabic, "Why the celebration?"

"We see our Caliph only once a year. Today is that day, because it is the feast of El-id-bed-Ramazan," he told me.

The Caliph was riding on a mule and was dressed in splendid royal robes of gold and silver. He was wearing a turban with precious stones, which was partially covered by a black scarf.

Again, I had a question for the old gentleman: "Why a black scarf—a sign of mourning—on this day of joy?"

"The black scarf," he told me, "is there to say that this splendor and these riches will be covered by darkness on the day of death."

When the crowd saw the Caliph, followed by a long retinue of all the lords of Islam, the princes of Arabia, the people grew excited and their singing increased. Men and women sang and danced before the Caliph and saluted him: "Peace be upon you, our Lord the King, Light of the Muslims." And he returned their greeting by kissing the hem of his robe.

The GOLDEN CAGE
The JEWS of KHEIBAR
The TOWER of BABEL

*L*ater that day, my host in the Jewish community told me how righteous and benevolent the Caliph is. "He cares about his subjects. He built a hospital and he pays for all sick people's medical assistance."

"I heard," I said, "that he keeps his own family prisoner. Why would a benevolent and righteous man do that?"

My host answered, "Once, a caliph was assassinated by his very own brothers. Then one of them became Caliph. After that, a law was passed that a caliph's family would live in luxury in their own palaces, in chains and under guard. We call this the Golden Cage. That way, future caliphs would never be assassinated."

In Baghdad I learned about the Jews of Kheibar, in Arabia. They are the only Jews who live in freedom, in their own land, and have no foreign ruler. They are said to be fierce warriors. I very much wanted to see them for myself. But to get to Kheibar is a long and dangerous journey through uninhabited deserts. Because of the extreme difficulty of finding a large, well-armed caravan, I reluctantly had to give up my desire to go there.

So, after leaving Baghdad, I went south instead to the Euphrates River to visit the ancient city of Babylon.

Remember the King of Babylon, the mighty Nebuchadnezzar, who set fire to and destroyed the first Temple in Jerusalem, and before whom everyone trembled in fear? His once magnificent palace is in ruins. Now only serpents and scorpions live there.

As I continued my journey along the Euphrates River, I also saw the remains of the Tower of Babel. I thought of the story in the Bible of how the Lord got angry when people in their arrogance tried to build a tower to reach heaven, and how He stopped them. Since everybody spoke one language, He confounded them and made them speak different languages. When one man asked for bricks, another brought him straw; when one asked for water, the other brought him sand. Then fire fell from heaven and split the tower to its very foundation.

SUSA
WHY DOES *the* PROPHET DANIEL'S COFFIN HANG *from a* BRIDGE?

I decided to go to the city of Susa, in Persia, because I had heard the great prophet Daniel was buried there.

Susa is divided by a river. As I was crossing the river, I noticed a coffin suspended by iron chains from the middle of the bridge. I couldn't believe my eyes. I was told, "This is the coffin of the prophet Daniel, peace be upon him."

The story goes that on one side of the river there lived rich merchants. And on their side was the tomb of the prophet Daniel. On the other side of the river were poor farmers. The poor became jealous. They said, "The rich became rich because the prophet Daniel is buried on their side of the river." The poor farmers demanded that the coffin be placed on their side of the river. But the rich refused. This led to a war

between the two sides. It lasted for quite some time. When the two sides grew tired, they became wiser. They made an agreement that they would take turns keeping Daniel's coffin, one year at a time. So they did, and both sides grew rich.

One day the King of Persia came to visit the city. When he heard that Daniel's coffin was going back and forth from one side of the river to the other, he said, "This is a disgrace to the prophet's memory." He ordered that the coffin be suspended from the exact middle of the bridge, and that at that very spot a house of prayer be built. It must be open to all who wished to pray, regardless of their religion. No fisherman might catch fish within a mile of the coffin, out of respect for the prophet.

Susa is the biblical Shushan, which in the prophet Daniel's day was under the rule of the Babylonians. Daniel was the only one capable of interpreting the dreams of the King of Babylon and the writing on the wall of the palace predicting the fall of Babylon, which happened when it was conquered by the Persians. Their King, in turn, honored Daniel. But the King's ministers were jealous and plotted against Daniel. And so the King was forced to have him thrown into the lions' den. But Daniel was unharmed because of divine protection.

Fights over the remains of holy men were common in the Middle Ages.

AMADIA
A FALSE MESSIAH

I continued north through the kingdom of Persia, to the province of Amadia near the Caspian Sea. There the Jewish communities had been praying for centuries for a messiah to come and lead them back to the Land of Israel. Ten years before my visit to Amadia, there was a man named David Alroy. He came to the Jewish people in Amadia and said, "I am the Messiah you have been praying for. God, blessed be He, has sent me to liberate you from the King of Persia, and to conquer Jerusalem, so that we can return." There were some who believed him and called him "our Messiah." He had studied, under the greatest teachers in Baghdad, the religious and secular scriptures of Judaism and Islam. He was also skilled in magic and in sorcery.

When the King of Persia heard that Alroy and his followers were planning a rebellion against him, he sent for Alroy. This didn't intimidate Alroy, and he went to the royal court without fear. When he arrived, the King asked, "Are you the King of the Jews?"

Alroy said, "I am."

So the King flew into a violent rage that a subject of his should dare call himself King before him. He commanded that Alroy be arrested and thrown into prison, from which no one ever got out alive.

Three days later the King was discussing with his ministers what to do with Alroy's followers. Suddenly Alroy appeared. The King demanded, "Who has released you?"

Alroy replied, "My own cunning. I'm not afraid of you, or of your slaves."

The King ordered his servants to seize him.

The servants said, "We don't see him—we only hear his voice."

Alroy said calmly, "I'm going," and now everybody saw him leave.

The King shouted, "Don't let him get away!"

The King, his ministers, and his servants went after Alroy. They followed him to the river. There they saw Alroy take off his cloak, spread it on the water, and cross the river on it. The King and his servants chased him in small boats but couldn't catch him. They were amazed and said, "There is no other magician like this man."

Alroy went to his people in Amadia and told them what had happened. They marveled at his cunning.

Then the King sent a threat to the head of all the Jewish communities in Baghdad to stop Alroy and his rebellion in Amadia, or else he'd kill all the Jews in his kingdom. Word spread quickly of the King's threat. The head of the Jewish communities sent a letter to Alroy, saying, "You are not the Messiah. Stop your rebellion or you'll be banned from the community." But Alroy refused.

To help the King of Persia, one of his vassals came up with a scheme. He sent for Alroy's father-in-law and gave him a bribe of ten thousand gold pieces to kill Alroy in secret. So the father-in-law went to Alroy's house and killed him while he was asleep. That was the end of Alroy's rebellion.

The King, however, was still angry, and he threatened to take revenge on the Jews of his kingdom. Eventually he was appeased by a bribe of one hundred thousand gold pieces. After that, there was no more talk of vengeance.

From the PERSIAN GULF to the RED SEA
OVENS of the EARTH

After traveling throughout Persia, I decided to go to Africa and see Egypt— Egypt, the ancient land of the Pharaohs, where the Israelites lived in bondage, and where they built the Pyramids, until Moses led them to freedom and the promised land.

I headed south to the Persian Gulf, where I embarked on a ship. Our first stop was El-Qatif on the Persian Gulf, where men fish for pearls. From there we continued through the Arabian Sea to Aden, and then to Zebid on the Red Sea.

The ovens of the earth must be in this part of the world. In Tudela, when the wind blows, it cools you. There, when the wind blows, it feels as if tongues of fire are licking your face. I hid belowdecks during the long days, in spite of the nauseating smells. At night I went on deck for a breath of air and a view of the starry skies.

The brightest spots on this sea voyage, besides the stars in the sky, were the stories about faraway places from travelers who went there. One traveler told me about a land I'd never heard of before, called China. To get there took a very long, dangerous voyage to the farthest East. One had to cross the Sea of Ning-pa, which was extremely stormy. Sometimes the winds were so fierce that the helmsman would lose control, and the ship would be swept into shallow waters. There it would stick fast. When the food ran out, the men would die.

So the sailors devised a way to avoid certain death. They would take along a supply of waterproof ox hides. If they were trapped in the sea of Ning-pa, a sailor armed with a knife would put on a skin to look like an animal and jump into the sea. An enormous bird called a griffin would mistake him for prey, pluck him out of the sea, and carry him to dry land to eat him. Once onshore, the sailor would kill the bird with his knife, and thus live to tell the tale.

CHINA
The LAND at the END of the WORLD

Benjamin was the first European to mention the existence of China, which he called Tsin.

The DESERT
BONE PILES, BIBLICAL PLAGUE, AMBUSH, TREACHEROUS SANDS *of the* SAHARA

When we reached the coast of Africa, I disembarked. Now I had to continue through the Eastern, or Arabian, Desert. Desert travel is hard on people and animals. It requires many preparations. I took biscuits for myself, straw for the camel, skins filled with water, and lemons.

It's essential to join a large, well-armed caravan in order to withstand bandit attacks. That is what I did.

The desert days were hot and the nights were cold. We began our journey at sundown. Using the stars as our guide, we traveled all night. Every now and then we came across piles of bones of donkeys, horses, and camels—a bit upsetting, to say the least. We slept during the day.

Traveling through the desert, I wished I were still on the ship. But riding a camel resembles being on a ship. At first I felt seasick. In order not to reveal my European identity, I had to keep my discomfort to myself and pretend I was used to riding a camel, just like any native. It took me a few days to get used to it.

When daybreak came, after a hard night's ride, I lay down to sleep but was soon awakened by sharp pains all over my body. Like a biblical plague, a swarm of insects, each twice the size of a fly, had come out of the sands and decided to have me for breakfast. Sleeping was out of the question. I was in pain the rest of the day, and all that night. Luckily, I was able to apply the juice from the lemons to my wounds, which speeded the healing.

As we continued our journey, we encountered a small group of people who were barefoot and walking with great effort. Their feet were bleeding. We shared our food and water with them.

They told us, "We were ambushed. In the flatness of the desert, a man was lying in wait. He was hiding behind a stone, buried in sand up to his shoulders, with his head showing. We didn't see him until it was too late. When he spotted our small, poorly armed caravan, he yelled to his men. Suddenly they appeared as if from nowhere, charging us on horseback. They attacked with lightning speed. They robbed us of everything, including our camels. We were forced to continue on foot until our shoes wore out. Some of us died of thirst. Occasionally we found brackish water, but drinking it made our thirst worse. If we hadn't met you, we, too, would be dead."

We invited them to join our caravan.

One night the winds began to rise. Sand and dust blew into our eyes, mouths, and ears. We could barely see what was in front of us. The animals were stumbling and had great difficulty advancing. We dismounted and walked on, leading the camels. Our eyes and throats were on fire. We were very thirsty. Luckily, the storm didn't last long.

The leader of the rescued caravan, who was walking by my side, said, "This storm was bad enough. But it didn't kill you, whereas winds in the Sahara Desert can. I once made a trip through the Sahara, hoping to reach Zawilah in Fezzan. I'd heard that caravans come to Zawilah poor and return rich. But the price of these riches is very high. In the Sahara are mountains of sand. When the wind rises, the sand can bury entire caravans and kill everybody. I never reached Zawilah, and I didn't get rich. But, Allah be praised, I was granted a priceless gift—I returned alive."

When we reached the Nile River, I left the caravan and took a boat to Cairo. As we sailed down the Nile, I could see the Pyramids in the distance. They looked like large man-made mountains. Near the Pyramids was the house where Moses, of blessed memory, would pray before going to demand that Pharaoh free the Israelites from bondage.

On a moonless night, our boat glided silently over the dark waters of the Nile. As we went around a bend in the river, there was a sudden burst of lights and the silhouette of a city. "Is the city on fire?" I asked.

"Cairo. You'll see," said the boat pilot mysteriously.

When we disembarked, I understood what the pilot meant. Unlike the cities of Europe, which are dark after sunset, Cairo was ablaze with countless torches lining the streets. Men squatted at the sides of the streets, talking peacefully in the coolness of the night. Others slept on mats on the ground in front of their shops.

The next morning I rose early. It was already terribly hot. Many streets were so narrow that the tops of the houses touched each other, providing some welcome shade. I passed by merchants leading camels and donkeys with heavy loads. Women with black veils over their faces with small holes for their eyes hurried to the shops and markets before midday, when the heat gets even worse.

CAIRO
The NILE
FEAST *or* FAMINE

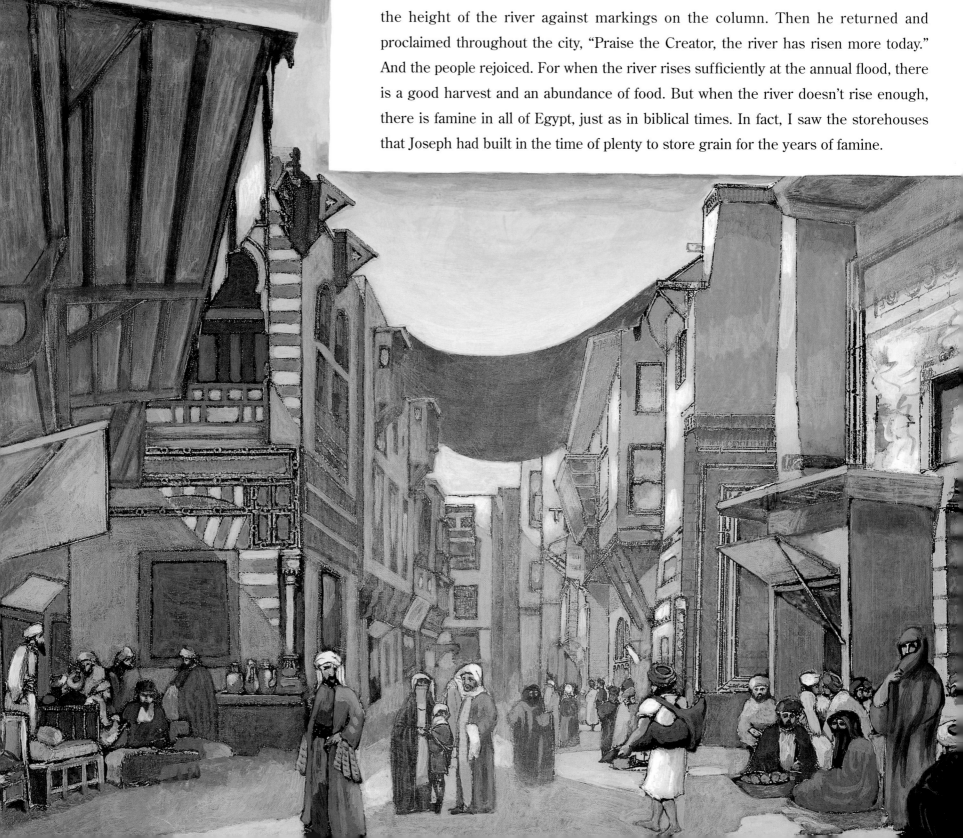

According to the Bible, Joseph was sold into slavery by his jealous brothers. In Egypt, Joseph interpreted Pharaoh's dream when no one else could. Joseph became a high official in Pharaoh's court.

Water is precious in Cairo, because it never rains or snows. The only source of water is the Nile. Vendors were everywhere selling water. They carried water in large containers with linen spouts. City workers sprinkled water on the streets to settle the dust.

As I stood on the banks of the Nile, I noticed a boat approaching an island in the middle of the river, where a marble column stood. An official from the boat measured the height of the river against markings on the column. Then he returned and proclaimed throughout the city, "Praise the Creator, the river has risen more today." And the people rejoiced. For when the river rises sufficiently at the annual flood, there is a good harvest and an abundance of food. But when the river doesn't rise enough, there is famine in all of Egypt, just as in biblical times. In fact, I saw the storehouses that Joseph had built in the time of plenty to store grain for the years of famine.

I didn't want to leave Egypt without seeing Mount Sinai, where Moses received the Ten Commandments from God. From Cairo, I continued by ship on the Nile to Alexandria, where I joined a caravan. We traveled through the Sinai Desert for eleven days. During this journey, I thought of the Israelites wandering through this very desert for forty years. We reached Mount Sinai on the twelfth day. You can imagine how moved I was to stand where the Israelites stood nearly 2,500 years ago. Now there is a large monastery of Syrian monks on the mountainside.

MOUNT SINAI
The TEN COMMANDMENTS

The LONG JOURNEY HOME

The journey to Mount Sinai and back to Alexandria took me nearly a month. The years of travel had begun to take their toll. I was tired. I was ready to return home. I'd begun to dress once more in European clothes, which I had kept with me. After resting for a couple of weeks in Alexandria, I boarded a ship bound for Sicily.

The weather was pleasing. The winds were in our favor. I looked forward to being back in Tudela—to see you all, to tell you where I'd been and all I'd seen, and to write a book about it. And so the first week passed peacefully.

Suddenly there came fierce winds, howling and raging. Our ship began to spin in circles. The winds tore the sails. The rudder broke. The ship began to take on water. The crew threw cargo overboard to lighten the load.

We helped the crew bail out the water. We worked frantically until we couldn't do any more.

The storm began to ease, but without sails and rudder our ship drifted helplessly. Then we hit rocks, and the ship cracked and began to break into pieces. We were sinking. We grabbed pieces of wood and floated on them until we reached an island. There we were stranded. The only food we could find in this deserted place was prickly plants. Out of desperation, we chewed on them to ease our hunger pangs.

I was so sick that I lost track of time. I don't know how long I was there. With God's help, a ship rescued us and took us to Sicily. After that experience, Sicily was like a vision of paradise. As soon as I got my strength back, I made my way safely home to Tudela.

HOME

In 1492, about three hundred years after Benjamin's return to Tudela, tragedy befell the Jews of Spain, their home for almost fifteen hundred years, when Queen Isabella and King Ferdinand, influenced by the Inquisition, expelled the Jews from Spain.

When I left Tudela fourteen years ago, my beard was black; now it's gray. Oh, how good and pleasing it is to sit with family and friends after all this time.

I've traveled far, and I've been to many lands, and I've seen what it's like to live under foreign rulers and to be subject to their whims. So far, we've been lucky in Tudela—first under the Muslims, and now under the Christians—but who knows how long that will last.

God be praised!

AUTHOR'S NOTE

In the days when travel was difficult and dangerous, returning alive from a voyage was in itself an accomplishment. The greatest medieval Jewish traveler, Benjamin of Tudela, having traveled through much of the then-known world in the twelfth century, not only returned home safely but also wrote about his journey in his *Book of Travels*. The book, written in Hebrew, is rich in facts and has little fiction, as was the way with travelers of his day. He was the first European to talk about the Assassins, and to mention the existence of a faraway, mysterious land called China. Besides his book, nothing personal is known about Benjamin, except that he was the son of Jonah and that he was a native of Tudela, in northern Spain.

Book of Travels was written in a matter-of-fact style and says nothing about the conditions or dangers he must have had to face during his fourteen-year journey. (My estimate of the length of his journey is based on the *Encyclopedia Judaica*.) The world through which he traveled was far from peaceful. But Benjamin doesn't mention the bloody massacres of his Jewish brethren that took place sixty and twelve years before he set out on his journey, by Christian Crusaders on their way to the Holy Land. Nor does he talk about the war between Crusaders and Muslims in the Near East, through which he traveled. He also says nothing of the persecution of Jews and Christians by Almohad Muslims in southern Spain. He does, however, allude to the oppression of Jews in Persia in his story about the false Messiah, David Alroy.

His factual but impersonal reporting, so helpful to historians of the Middle Ages, presents some problems if one wishes to write about Benjamin's travels in a way that might appeal to young readers. Since my goal was to retell his journey, and to give young readers a glimpse of what travel and living conditions were like in medieval times, I had to take certain liberties. I tried to invent as little as possible, however, and to be as faithful as possible, if not to the letter of Benjamin's book, at least to its spirit. In order to personalize the narrative, I've taken the liberty of retelling his travels in the first person. In that spirit, I filled in the travel conditions, which Benjamin's book lacks, by using the experiences and incidents that did happen to other medieval travelers, rather than invent my own. For the convenience of the young reader, I used modern names wherever possible. When questions arose whether Benjamin's narrative was based on an actual visit or on hearsay, I consulted the Hebrew text. For example, whereas translations state "*here* dwell the Jews called Kheibar," as if Benjamin is reporting what he saw, the Hebrew text says "and *there* dwell the Jews called Kheibar," suggesting that he had heard about them rather than that he had actually gone there.

Concerning my illustrations: while researching sources for pictorial reference, I found relatively few pictures from Benjamin's time that lent themselves to my project. Consequently, I supplemented what I found from the twelfth and earlier centuries with pictures from later medieval periods as well, or, as a last resort, drawing on my findings, I relied on my imagination to fill in the gaps. My aim was to convey primarily a feeling of what it might have been like in Benjamin's day.

BIBLIOGRAPHY

Adler, Elkan Nathan, ed. *Jewish Travellers in the Middle Ages: 19 Firsthand Accounts*. New York: Dover Publications, 1987.

Allom, Thomas. *Istanbul: From the Past until Today*. Istanbul: Keskin Color Kartpostalcilik, n.d.

Benjamin, Sandra. *The World of Benjamin of Tudela: A Medieval Mediterranean Travelogue*. Madison, N.J.: Fairleigh Dickinson University Press, 1995.

Benjamin of Tudela. *Sefer ha-Massaoth (Book of Travels)*. In Eisenstein, *Ozar Massaoth*.

"The Circular Voyage of Rabbi Petahia of Regensburg." In Eisenstein, *Ozar Massaoth*.

Comte, Suzanne. *Everyday Life in the Middle Ages*. Trans. David Macrae. Geneva, Switzerland: Editions Minerva, 1978.

de Lange, Nicholas, ed. *The Illustrated History of the Jewish People*. New York and San Diego: Harcourt Brace, 1997.

Department of Education, Israel. *Journey to the Past, from the Middle Ages to the Modern Era*. Israel, n.d.

Eisenstein, J. D., ed. *Ozar Massaoth: A Collection of Itineraries by Jewish Travelers to Palestine, Syria, Egypt . . . Pilgrimage to Holy Tombs and Sepulchres*. Tel Aviv: n.p., 1969.

Encyclopaedia Britannica, 1966, 1976.

Encyclopedia Judaica. Jerusalem: Keter Publications, 1971.

Evans, Joan, ed. *The Flowering of the Middle Ages*. New York: Bonanza Books, 1966.

Gardiner, Robert, ed. *Cogs, Caravels and Galleons: The Sailing Ship 1000–1650*. London: Conway Maritime Press, 1994.

Goitein, S. D., ed. and trans. *Letters of Medieval Jewish Traders*. Princeton, N.J.: Princeton University Press, 1973.

Graetz, Professor H. *Popular History of the Jews*. New York: Hebrew Publishing Co., 1919.

Grayzel, Solomon. *A History of the Jews*. Philadelphia: The Jewish Publication Society of America, 1947.

Holmes, Urban Tigner, Jr. *Daily Living in the Twelfth Century: Based on the Observations of Alexander Neckam in London and Paris*. Madison: University of Wisconsin Press, 1952.

The Jewish Encyclopedia. New York, Ktav Publishing House.

Letter of Travel of R. Meshullam ben Menahem of Volterra. In Eisenstein, *Ozar Massaoth*.

Metzger, Therese and Mendel. *Jewish Life in the Middle Ages: Illuminated Hebrew Manuscripts of the Thirteenth to the Sixteenth Centuries*. Secaucus, N.J.: Chartwell Books, 1982.

Mundy, John H., and Peter Riesenberg. *The Medieval Town*. Princeton, N.J.: D. Van Nostrand Co., 1958.

The New Standard Jewish Encyclopedia. New York: Facts on File, 1992.

Ohler, Norbert. *The Medieval Traveller*. Woodbridge, Suffolk, England: Boydell Press, 1989.

The Oxford Dictionary of Byzantium. Oxford and New York: Oxford University Press, 1991.

Pirenne, Henri. *Economic and Social History of Medieval Europe*. New York: Harcourt Brace, 1937.

Prawer, Joshua. *Description of Travel in Eretz-Israel during the Crusades*. Israel: Cathedra, 1987.

Routes of Sepharad. Cáceres, Spain: Rectorado de la Universidad de Extremadura, n.d.

Rowling, Marjorie. *Everyday Life of Medieval Travellers*. New York: G. P. Putnam's Sons, 1971.

Saalman, Howard. *Medieval Cities*. New York: George Braziller, 1968.

Signer, Michael A. *The Itinerary of Benjamin of Tudela: Travels in the Middle Ages*. Malibu, Calif.: Joseph Simon/Pangloss Press, 1987.

Singman, Jeffrey L. *Daily Life in Medieval Europe*. Westport, Conn.: Greenwood Publishing Group, 1999.

Tate, Georges. *The Crusaders: Warriors of God*. New York: Harry N. Abrams, 1996.

Three Letters of Travel of Rabbi Ovadiah of Bartenura. In Eisenstein, *Ozar Massaoth*.

HOWE LIBRARY
13 E. SOUTH ST.
HANOVER, NH 03755

DEC 2 1 2007